BILL THE

ar

by

W·HEATH ROBINSON

edited by Timothy Forder

B ill the Minder looked after his cousins, Boadicea and Chad. They wandered with him everywhere. Even in his dreams.

And having dreamed up so many people, places and things, they all went home. Boadicea and Chad returned to their mother, Chloe, who made them peanut butter sandwiches and fresh orange juice.

Now, Chloe was, in a number of ways, a very remarkable person. She was capable of turning her hand to almost anything. She could take wonderful photographs, and mount them in an album. And she was very good at marquetry, that is, making pictures by using different types of wood. In fact, she was very accomplished at all sorts of useful things. But, unfortunately, whenever she went to get her sticky tape, her watering can, or her glue, it was never in its place. Boadicea or Chad had always borrowed it for some other purpose, and not returned it.

When she was gardening, they used her trowel

to dig potholes. And when she was cooking, they used her mixing bowls as helmets. And they never put anything back in its place.

Finally, Chloe could not stand it any longer. She threw down her tea towel, retired to her bedroom and gave way to tears. Chad locked himself in the bathroom

and would not come out, while Boadicea ran down to
the fields to fetch Bill.

Chloe, still somewhat agitated, outlined the
problem to Bill from the upstairs banisters:

'The wretched little vermin steal my things and

are too selfish to return them!'

    Bill mused over the facts for a moment, and then
came up with a very good idea. He attached every one
of Chloe's items to a length of fine fishing line, so that it
could be reeled in at a moment's notice.

    Bill tried the system and it seemed to work.

Then Old Crispin returned and kissed Chloe on the cheek, but it didn't seem to soothe her much.

So Bill slipped on his waistcoat, filled its pockets with all he might need for a trip and, to get Boadicea and Chad out of Chloe's way, he took them out on to the downs in search of fresh adventures.

THE DOCTOR

A nd as they wandered, they met the celebrated Dr Ebenezer Scrout. He looked extremely miserable. So Bill stopped and said,

'Why are you looking so sad?'

'Because,' said the eminent doctor, 'I have reached the time of life when one has to succeed in the things one sets out to do. But I haven't. I've failed.'

'Oh no,' said Boadicea. 'You can't have. You're the famous Dr Scrout.'

'Very true,' said the doctor, 'but I'm still a drivelling old failure.'

'I'm sure you're the finest doctor who ever was,' said Boadicea (or Chad or Bill).

'I'm an ineffective, futile, inept, ignorant, misguided, babbling old wash-out,' said the doctor.

'Aren't you a very good doctor, then, doctor?' asked Chad.

'No, I'm not. The point is,' sighed the prominent physician, 'I am a doctor with no one to cure.'

'Oh,' said Bill. 'That is a bit awkward.'

'It all started,' said the doctor, 'when I was a young practitioner. I had the splendid idea of adding to every prescription a small amount of my patients' favourite dish – chicken flavoured painkillers or salmon sleeping pills. I also developed a wonderful technique for giving injections, that made my patients swoon with delight. Everybody wanted to be ill, so that they could be prescribed my delightful remedies.

'I was having to work day and night. The streets became deserted and weeds began to grow between the

cracks in the pavements. Eventually, things grew so bad, I had to abandon my practice and here I am on the downs without a single patient.'

'Don't worry,' said Bill. 'We'll make people ill for you.' And he put together an incredible seasick-making machine called 'The Doctor's Friend'.

Dr Ebenezer was the first to try it out. In only a few moments the doctor was so ill, he had to make use of the paper bag provided. He was very impressed.

'With this,' he said, 'there will be any number of people who will require instant medical attention.'

And so they all set off across the downs in search of new patients for the renowned Dr Ebenezer Scrout.

THE SICILIAN CLEANING-LADY

And as they made their way across the downs Bill saw a woman waving her arms about and mumbling to herself in Italian.

'Is she ill?' asked the doctor hopefully.

'Vorrei raccontarti la mia storia,' she said, and began to tell her story, which Bill translated for those who could not understand Italian.

'I am a daughter of a Sicilian peasant, but I was educated in Florence at the school for professional house cleaners. When I had passed all my exams, I looked out for a suitable job and eventually found employment at the home of Mr and Mrs Pettigrew of Pimlico. Unfortunately, I soon discovered that the Pettigrews were rather unreasonable.

'They objected when I hung my certificate from the school of professional house cleaners beside the mediocre sketches of their precocious little son, Basil Herbert. They didn't like it when I forbade them to put their teacups down on my newly polished surfaces. And they moaned when I would not allow them to sit upon my freshly plumped up cushions. But worst of all, they hated it when I interrupted the little Herbert's singing lessons.'

'Singing lessons?' asked Chad.
'Si, si. E terribile. E orribile!'
'Perhaps,' said the persistent physician, 'It is not impossible that we might entice the amiable lady on to the "Doctor's Friend".'

'The minute the Pettigrews are out of the house,' the cleaning-lady went on, 'I spare no effort in trying to silence little Herbert's frightful warbling. I lock him in the bathroom with the bath taps running, hoping that this will drown the dreadful trill. But it doesn't.

'Then I feed him on plates and plates of spaghetti, thinking that this will be enough to choke the ghastly serenade. But it isn't. What shall I do?' she wailed.

'A brief spell on the "Doctor's Friend" might relieve the distressed lady's mind of her present predicament,' said the eminent physician.

Bill had a better idea. And he made a brilliant gadget for

removing the nuisance of Basil Herbert's singing. Bill listened very carefully in case he could still hear the odious Herbert's dirge. But he couldn't. The Sicilian cleaning-lady was delighted with the result. Mr and Mrs Pettigrew, less so. In fact, they sold their house in Pimlico and moved to somewhere in the north.

'Che cosa fare?' cried the Sicilian lady, for now she had no house to clean.

Boadicea felt so sorry for her she said, 'We're trying to find new patients for the celebrated Dr Scrout, would you like to come with us?' And they continued their amazing journey across the downs.

THE BUTTON CRANE OF BARABOO

Bill led the way and Boadicea held the doctor's hand. Suddenly they saw before them their friend, the very respectable gentleman. In a cage he was carrying the fabulously attractive green-toed button crane of Baraboo, called Norris.

As they approached him, they noticed that the dignified gentleman appeared to be rather pale and agitated.

So Bill went up to him and said,
'What's the matter?'
But the good man simply held up the wonderful green-toed button crane, and said in a low voice,
'Norris belches.'
'Oh dear,' said Bill.
'Yes, it happens every time I give him a Peruvian yap bean, of which, incidentally, he is inordinately fond.'
And he held up the cage again and said sadly, 'Norris is a foul fowl.'

So Boadicea brought forward the remarkable Dr
Scrout, who was pleased to find a new patient to attend.
He inspected the aristocratic animal from every angle,
and eventually wrote out a prescription, which Boadicea
went to fetch from the chemist. Then, she gave a
spoonful of the liquid to the bird. And Bill offered him a
Peruvian yap bean, and they waited to see what would
happen.

But, unfortunately, the renowned doctor's linctus proved unsuccessful. Which Chad found rather amusing.

Then the Sicilian cleaning-lady said,
'Ho qualcosa del dare el bel bambino.' And she gave the exotic creature a spoonful of her own Sicilian remedy.

And Bill offered him another Peruvian yap bean, and they waited to see what would be the result. But, unfortunately, the kind woman's medicine also proved ineffective, which Chad found highly entertaining.

The puzzled Dr Scrout rubbed his chin. The Sicilian cleaning-lady said, 'Che cosa faremo?' And the respectable gentleman began to grow paler and more agitated than ever.

So Bill, rather cleverly, put together a device for curing the enchanting Norris of his belching.

When Norris was back in his cage, Bill gave him another yap bean and they waited to see if there was any improvement. The doctor was hopeful. The Sicilian cleaning-lady was delighted. The respectable gentleman was relieved. And Bill was triumphant.

All was silent. But not for long. Suddenly, from his rear end, Norris emitted a sound far worse than a belch – and the respectable gentleman fainted.

THE WAITER

After they had travelled a short distance the Sicilian woman began to lag behind, until, finally, she sat down on a tree trunk and refused to walk another step.

So Bill went up to her and said, 'What's the matter?'

But the woman just looked sad and wouldn't speak.

Boadicea poured her a hot cup of tea, and she began to explain her problem.

'When I was last in Florence, I went into a cafe to have some supper. I was given the menu by a charming young waiter, who told me that he thought I must be the most beautiful woman in all of Italy. And when he came to me with my capuccino, he touched my arm and said, "I think I am in love with you."'

'After I left Florence,' the woman went on, 'I thought I would never see him again. But this morning I had a letter. It was from my waiter. I was so happy!'

Now, the waiter had written a lot of nice things about how well they were suited, how terribly he had missed her and how desperately he wanted to see her again. But, unfortunately, the very corner where he had written his address was torn away.

'You see,' she wailed, 'How can I reply when I don't have his address?'

'Where exactly did you lose it?' asked Bill.

And she pointed to the precise spot.

As she did so, she leant over, revealing the vital piece of paper caught in her stocking top. Bill turned to Boadicea and said, 'Boadicea, would you tell her?'

And Boadicea turned to Chad and said, 'Chad, would you tell her?'

And Chad turned to them both and said, 'No!'

So Bill rigged up a series of mirrors to enable the Sicilian cleaning-lady to locate the missing address for herself. And soon a reply was on its way to her eager Italian waiter.

Unfortunately, when he arrived, he was not quite as she remembered him. But she didn't seem to mind.

And as it was getting rather late, Bill, Boadicea and Chad left them and hurried back home across the downs.

Dragon
Grafton Books
A Division of the Collins Publishing Group
8 Grafton Street, London W1X 3LA

Published by Dragon Books

ISBN 0 583 31085 0

Printed and bound in Great Britain by Ancient House Press

Set in Bembo

If you have enjoyed Bill the Minder and want to join
him and his friends helping other children in need – send
your donation to:
The NSPCC, Dept. 68319, 67 Saffron Hill, London EC1N 8RS.